KU-726-197

Jerry the Giant

Cousin Cuthbert

Auntie Alice

The Shopkeeper

Great Aunt Winifred

OXFORD
UNIVERSITY PRESS

Great Clarendon Street, Oxford OX2 6DP

Oxford University Press is a department of the University of Oxford.
It furthers the University's objective of excellence in research, scholarship,
and education by publishing worldwide. Oxford is a registered trade mark of
Oxford University Press in the UK and in certain other countries

Text copyright © Oxford University Press 2009, 2010, 2012
Illustrations copyright © Korky Paul 2009, 2010, 2012, 2017
The moral rights of the author and illustrator have been asserted
The characters in this work are the original creation of Valerie Thomas who
retains copyright in the characters

Database right Oxford University Press (maker)

Winnie and Wilbur: Winnie the Twit first published as Winnie the Twit in 2009
Winnie and Wilbur: Giddy-Up Winnie first published as Giddy-Up Winnie
in 2009
Winnie and Wilbur: Winnie on Patrol first published as Winnie on Patrol in 2010
Winnie and Wilbur: Disgusting Dinners and Other Stories first published as
Totally Winnie! in 2012
This edition first published in 2017

The stories are complete and unabridged

All rights reserved. No part of this publication may be reproduced,
stored in a retrieval system, or transmitted, in any form or by any means,
without the prior permission in writing of Oxford University Press,
or as expressly permitted by law, or under terms agreed with the appropriate
reprographics rights organization. Enquiries concerning reproduction
outside the scope of the above should be sent to the Rights Department,
Oxford University Press, at the address above

You must not circulate this book in any other binding or cover
and you must impose this same condition on any acquirer

British Library Cataloguing in Publication Data: data available

ISBN: 978-0-19-275893-4

1 3 5 7 9 10 8 6 4 2
Printed in Great Britain

Paper used in the production of this book is a natural,
recyclable product made from wood grown in sustainable forests.
The manufacturing process conforms to the environmental
regulations of the country of origin.

Winnie AND Wilbur

DISGUSTING DINNERS
and
other
stories

EAST SUSSEX COUNTY COUNCIL
WITHDRAWN

2 3 AUG 2024

04449290

Wilbur

Winnie the Witch

Doctor Which

The Little Ordinaries

Uncle Owen

Mrs Parmar

LAURA OWEN & KORKY PAUL

Winnie AND Wilbur

DISGUSTING DINNERS

and other stories

OXFORD
UNIVERSITY PRESS

CONTENTS

WINNIE'S
Wheels

Yawn! went Winnie standing in her sloth slippers, watching raindrops slide down the window like baby snails.

'It's raining, it's pouring,
my cat is snoring.
This is so blooming
boring, boring, boring!'

Winnie put fingers on two different raindrops on the other side of the window. She followed the drops downwards to see which drop would win.

'Drippy-drop won!' she said. Wilbur
opened one eye, then closed it again, and
yawned widely, showing his fangs.

Winnie took a pongberry from the fruit
bowl and she threw it at Wilbur.

'Mrrow!'

'Let's *do* something!' said Winnie.
'I know, I'll ring Jerry next door and see if
he'd like to come and play Crocodile Snap
or Crabbage.'

But, 'I'm just packin' to go on
holiday, missus,' said Jerry down the
telling moan. 'Toodle pip.'

'Holiday?!' said Winnie. 'A holiday,
Wilbur! That's exactly what we need.
We'll get away for a nice holiday!'

Suddenly Winnie had energy again.
'Abracadabra!'

11

A pile of holiday brochures landed on
the table. Winnie pounced on them.

'Come on, Wilbur! Help me choose!'

Winnie found holidays by the sea.

'Lovely!' said Winnie.

'Mrrow!' said Wilbur.

'You've had enough of wetness from all
this rain, have you?' said Winnie. 'This
one looks dry!' she said, waving a picture
of an African plain with lions prowling.

12

'Meeeow!' squeaked Wilbur.

'Don't you like cats that big?' said Winnie. 'Where do you want to go, then?'

Wilbur pointed at a holiday for old people which showed a fat cat lying snoozing in front of a fire.

'That'd be about as exciting as watching the Snail Olympics!' said Winnie.

ΔΙΑΚΟΠΕΣ ΣΤΑ ΚΥΘΗΡΑ

'Oh, dear! Perhaps I should just leave
you with my sister Wanda and her cat
Wayne while I go on holiday on my own?'

'MRRRROW!' said Wilbur, his eyes
opening wide and his claws clinging
tightly to the tatty rat-leather chair he was
sitting on.

'Oh, all right! Don't get your whiskers
in a whizz!' said Winnie. 'I'd rather have a

holiday with you. But where can we go where we'll both be happy?' Then—

zing!—'I've got it!' she said. 'Let's go on a mystery tour!'

'Meeow?' said Wilbur.

'You know,' said Winnie. 'A journey where we just set off and keep going until we find somewhere we like. Then we stop and enjoy it.'

Wilbur did a claws-up sign, so that was decided.

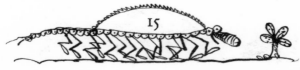

Winnie got packing.

'Elephant snorkel and seal flippers in case we go in the sea. A bunny-bonnet hat and skunk boots in case we find snow. Squashed-fly biscuits and best mouldy-oldy cheese and radish-reptile relish in case we don't like the food when we get there. Midge attraction cream, crocodile bite lotion, a waiter-charming potion, pig crackling oinkment for sunburn. A tent and pegs and matches and pans and . . . oh,' said Winnie. 'This bag isn't going to be anywhere near big enough.'

Winnie filled a suitcase too, and a trunk. Then Wilbur came staggering along with his backpack full of fish-fin bits and his comfy-wumfy blanket and his sun

glasses and his goggles and his maps and
his tin opener and his whisker cream.

'Pile it all in, Wilbur!' said Winnie.
'We'll manage somehow!'

They staggered outside with their
luggage, and were instantly soaked.

'Tut! That's another thing!' said
Winnie, running back inside.
'I forgot my umbrella and my
smelly-wellies!'

They climbed onto Winnie's broomstick.
'Off we go, Broom!' shouted Winnie.
'Take us wherever you like! Oooo, this is
exciting! I wonder where we'll end up!'

Heave! went Broom. **Strain-tug-
heave!** Nothing moved.

The poor broomstick just couldn't lift such a weight of luggage. 'Well, we can't leave our luggage behind,' said Winnie. 'There's only one thing for it!' Winnie waved her wand, *swish-swish!*

'Abracadabra!'

And suddenly there was a car parked in front of her house.

'Oooo! Isn't it shiny! Isn't it handsome? And big! With a boot for the luggage! And a roof to keep the rain out! Why didn't I think of getting a car before?'

'Meeow!' agreed Wilbur.

Winnie began to throw luggage into the

20

boot, and tie it onto the roof, and hang it from the door handles. 'Hecking hippopotamus! We still need more room! I know what!' **Swish!** went Winnie's wand again.

'*Abracadabra!*'

And instantly there was a fine witch
caravan behind the car.

'Perfect!' said Winnie, throwing her
broomstick into the caravan. 'Now, we're
ready for anything! Get into the car, Wilbur!
I'll get the heating going, and the windscreen
vipers, then off we brolly well go!'

22

But Winnie didn't know her windscreen viper knob from her headlight dipper. She didn't know her gear stick from her brake pedal from her toad horn.

Suddenly there were lights flashing and horns honking and engines revving. Wilbur's fur was standing on end!

'Driving a car really can't be that difficult!' said Winnie, prodding a big button on the dashboard. 'Lots of idiots manage it!' **Lurch! Leap! St-st-st-stagger-stop!**

'It's like a blasted kangaroo!' said Winnie. 'Stupid thing!'

'MMMMMMMMmew!' whimpered Wilbur.

'What?' said Winnie. 'You want me to give up? Just one more try, eh?'

Prod, kick, turn, yank. Vrrroooom! The car lurched backwards this time, bumping the caravan—

thump-bump-lump-lump-lump!

'Oooooooer!' said Winnie. 'We're going backwards and the road only goes

forwards! Errr! Hold tight, Wilbur! We're
going dowwnnn the hiillll.' **Crump!**

'Oh,' said Winnie.

The car and caravan had come to a halt
beside the duck pond at the bottom of
Winnie's garden. Their wheels were
sinking into the mud, completely stuck.

'Oh,' said Winnie again.

25

Wilbur stepped out of the car. He was
trembling. His eyes were huge. Winnie took
one look at him. 'Er . . . Wilbur, shall we
just stay and have our holiday here?'

'Meeow!' said Wilbur, nodding fiercely.

The rain had stopped and the sun was
just coming out. Winnie and Wilbur set
up their tent and sorted their belongings.

'We can snorkel in the pond,' said

Winnie. 'We can climb that tree! We can do anything we blooming well want to do!'

They toasted marsh-smellows over the stove. 'We've got all our favourite things!' said Winnie. 'And when it's time to go home, we don't even have to drive there!'

'Meeow!' said Wilbur, wiping a paw across his forehead.

'It's almost perfect!' said Winnie.
'All that's missing is a bit of company.'

Then suddenly there was a **THUD THUD THUDDING** sound and,
'Hullo, missus!' said a voice.

'Jerry!' said Winnie. 'I thought you were going on holiday!'

'I've gone!' said Jerry. 'I *is* on holiday. Look at what I'm wearin'!'

'Then come and join us for a drinky-goo, Jerry,' said Winnie. 'And then we'll have a mudcastle making competition—you and Scruff against me and Wilbur.'

So they did. Who do you think was the winner?

Blooming
WINNIE

Squeaky-squeaky-squeak-eek!

'Who's maddening a mouse?' said Winnie,
looking up from her breakfast toast and
mildew marmalade spread. 'Oh, it's my
blooming mobile moan! Have you been
playing with the ringtones again, Wilbur?'
Winnie snatched the phone from her
pocket and put it to her ear. 'Hello?'

A ladylike voice on the phone said,
'This is Mrs Parmar from the school.
I have a favour to ask.'

31

'Oh, yes?' said Winnie.

'Yes,' said Mrs Parmar. 'Could the schoolchildren come and look at plants and creatures in your garden, Winnie? They're doing a project.'

'Oooo, that'd be lovely!' said Winnie. 'Little ordinaries in my garden!'

'There is one rule!' said Mrs Parmar sternly.

'What's that then?' said Winnie.

'You must absolutely do absolutely no magic at all while the children are absolutely with you.'

'Easy-peasy pink-worm-squeezy!' said Winnie.

'I'm trusting you, Winnie!' said Mrs Parmar. 'I'll bring the children at two o'clock.'

'Yippee!' said Winnie, trying to dance with Wilbur. Then she looked out of the window. 'Oh,' she said. 'Ooo, dear. I'd forgotten what a tangle-mangle the garden is.' Winnie began to pull her wand from her sleeve. 'Mrs P didn't say, "No magic *before* the little ordinaries arrive". Let's do some wand-gardening, Wilbur!'

Wilbur followed her outside.

'Children will want frilly-flowery, sweet-smelly, bright-colouredy kinds of things,' said Winnie, waving her wand.

'Abracadabra!'

And instantly Winnie was wearing
the most frilly-flowery, sweet-smelly,
bright-colouredy shoes you've ever seen.

'Blooming bats' bottoms!' said Winnie.

'What's gone wrong?'

Wilbur sniggered behind a paw, and pointed at Winnie's wand. The wand was bent.

'It's pointing to the wrong blooming thing!' said Winnie. 'Let's try again! Abracadabra!'

And instantly the big black crows
sitting in the trees became frilly-flowery,
sweet-smelly, bright-colouredy birds.

'That's not right!' said Winnie, trying
to straighten her wand. But it just wilted
again. 'What in the witchy world is wrong
with my wand?'

Winnie tried stroking the wand. 'Don't oo feel very well, wandy?' The wand stayed wilted. Winnie bandaged the wand. She dipped the wand in medicine. But it stayed wilted. 'I've run out of ideas,' said Winnie. 'Let's look in Great Aunt Winifred's *Book of All Things Magic* and see if she knows how to cure it.'

Winnie opened the dusty book and
looked at the spells inside.

'Oh, heck and botheration!' she said.
'I can't read this curly piggy tails kind of
writing! Oh, I wish my great auntie who
lived so long ago and was so wise could help
me. I was named after her, you know,
Wilbur, but I've never been as clever as her.'

'Buck yourself up, gal!' said a dusty old
voice. *Cough, cough!*

40

'Oooer!' said Winnie.

'Hisss!' went Wilbur, all prickles and big eyes.

Because there, looming like grey smog floating over the table, was Winnie's Great Aunt Winifred.

'What's your problem, gal?' she boomed.

'Ug. Er, gnn,' said Winnie who had forgotten how to talk.

'Spit it out!' said the spectre.

'It's my wand,' said Winnie. 'It's wilted.'

'Booster's wand food will soon sort it!' said Winifred.

'I've tried that,' said Winnie. 'I've tried everything! Nothing works!'

'Don't despair, gal,' said Great Aunt Winifred. 'Just grow yerself a new wand, don't-ya know.'

'Really?' said Winnie.

'As easy as picking fleas from a fairy cake,' said Winifred. 'Shove yer wand into some soil. Water it. Give it some sunshine. Watch it grow. Simple as that.'

'Cor,' said Winnie. 'I never knew.'

43

Winnie planted her wilted wand, and gave it water and sunshine, and it began to grow. It grew up and out, growing fat wands, thin wands, knobbly wands, curvy wands, wibbly-wobbly wands.

'Just pick one good straight one. That's the ticket!' said Great Aunt Winifred, floating just behind Winnie's right ear.

Winnie was just reaching out to pick a perfect wand, when they heard something.

'Sounds like a hundred screeching owl chicks, just popped from their eggs!' said Great Aunt Winifred, covering her ears.

'It's the little ordinaries!' said Winnie. 'Get into the house, Auntie! They mustn't see you!'

'Here are the children, Winnie!' said Mrs Parmar. 'I'll collect them at three o'clock. Have a good afternoon, and remember . . .'

'No magic!' said Winnie. 'I know.'

But the little ordinaries didn't seem to know about that rule. They weren't interested in the giant rhubarb and custard plant crawling with cattypillars. They weren't interested in stinking nettles or the tangle-vines or the bulging bugle bugs. No. The little ordinaries ran straight to the wand tree and began picking wands, and waving wands, and . . .

'Oh, I don't think . . .!' began Winnie,
but nobody was listening. 'Oh, dimpled
slug bottoms, whatever shall I do, Wilbur?
Wilbur?'

But Wilbur wasn't at Winnie's feet
any more. Instead there was a small
sad-looking black mammoth. 'Wilbur!'
cried Winnie in anguish. 'Oh, please
little ordinaries, don't . . .'

Zip! Zap! Ting! Splosh! Zob!

Magic was flying everywhere. Plants
were being changed. Children were being
changed. Winnie was being changed!

Then Great Aunt Winifred came
wafting to the rescue. She roared into
the garden like cross fog.

'Desist! At once!' she told the children in a voice that echoed from the house walls.

The children did desist. They froze, their mouths open.

'Place every wand on the ground!' boomed Winifred. 'Now, line up, two by two. Backs straight! No talking!'

Great Aunt Winifred picked up one good straight wand.

'Abracadabra!'

And instantly Winnie and Wilbur were back to being themselves. Just in time, because there was Mrs Parmar hurrying along to fetch the children.

'Oh, my goodness!' said Mrs Parmar when she saw the children. 'They *are* being well-behaved! You didn't do any magic on them, did you, Winnie?'

'*I've* not done any magic all afternoon,' said Winnie.

'Good!' said Mrs Parmar. 'Back to school then, children! My goodness, how quiet you are! Well done, Winnie!'

'Phew in a shrew stew!' said Winnie as the children disappeared. 'Shall we have a bonfire of all those wands?'

51

So Winnie and Wilbur and Great Aunt Winifred enjoyed a bonfire that burned every colour and sparked magical sounds and smells and spooks and surprises while they toasted squish-mellows.

At bedtime Winifred began to tell Winnie, 'Brush your hair one hundred strokes, gal! And put on a corset for bed or you'll end up with no figure! Have you polished . . .?'

'Time to go back in your book, Auntie,' said Winnie. 'Nighty-night. Mind the book worms don't bite!' She slammed it shut. And then there was silence.

'Ah!' said Winnie.

'Meeowwah!' agreed Wilbur.

WINNIE'S
Tea Party

Scrunch-flap-munch-crunch!

'The blooming letter box is scoffing
the post again. Quick!' shouted Winnie.

Wilbur leapt to rescue a postcard
dangling from the letter box's teeth.

'Let me see!' said Winnie. 'Ooo, look!
"Pyramids at sunset" from Cousin
Cuthbert. I haven't seen Cuthbert since ...
Ooo, Wilbur, let's invite him to tea!
And let's invite Uncle Owen and
Auntie Alice, too!'

Wilbur made a face.

'We'll send the invitations by parrot-post,' said Winnie. *Abracadabra!*

Instantly there were three parrots flapping and squawking all around the room, knocking everything over.

'Come and perch on my wand, parrots,' said Winnie. 'Shut your silly beaks and listen. You're to go to Cousin Cuthbert and Uncle Owen and Auntie Alice, and ask them all if they'd like to come for tea today. Flap-off, and bring me back the replies!'

With green, yellow, orange, and red
feathers flying everywhere, the birds flew
away. Winnie was just picking up feathers
and trying them in her hair when there
was a peck-peck sound at the door, and
three parrot voices saying, 'Open the
door, open the door, open the door.'

PECK
PECK
PECK

PECK
PECKPECK
PECK

58

'I think I'd better open the door,' said Winnie, and she let the parrots in.

'Cuthbert can come,' said the first parrot.

'Owen OK,' said the second.

'Auntie Alice accepts,' said the third.

'Goody!' said Winnie. 'They're all coming! I'd better get cooking!'

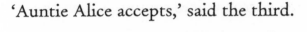

Winnie set to work. She thumped and squashed and pulled and squirted, and shoved lots of tins into the oven.

'Lots of lovely food,' said Winnie, licking a mixing spoon. 'Yum!'

Smoke rose from the oven behind her.

'Meow!' said Wilbur.

'Oh, wombat wellies!' said Winnie, grabbing the yeti fur oven mitt. The rhubarb and rat-tail buns weren't too badly burned, but Winnie was all of a fluster. As she swung round with her oven mitt—**thwack, crash, shatter!**

'Oh, no! The teapot's in pieces!' wailed Winnie. 'Whatever shall I do? You can't have a tea party without tea!'

Wilbur glanced at the clock.

'I know!' said Winnie. 'No time for shopping. I shall have to magic a new teapot. *Abracadabra!*'

And—**zing!**—there on the table was a beautiful big elephant teapot with a wavy trunk spout.

'Lovely!' said Winnie.

But when Winnie tried pouring tea from the trunk spout, it came out—**whoopsy-splosh**—jumping right over the cup to slosh on to the table.

'That's no blooming good!' said Winnie. 'Let's try again! *Abracadabra!*'

The next teapot's spout fell straight off, into the cup with the tea. The pot after that had its spout on a bit sideways so it poured tea to one side of the cup, all over the table and onto the floor. Winnie and Wilbur were wading in a sea of tea.

'Tea, tea everywhere, but not a drop to drink!' said Winnie. 'Blooming stupid magic!'

Grrrr-woof-ding-dong! nagged the dooryell. **Woof-ding!**

'Flipping fishcakes, they're here, Wilbur!'

Winnie patted down her hair and
hurried to open the door. 'Oh, do come
in, Uncle Owen and Auntie Alice and
Cousin Cuthbert.'

Winnie pushed them all into her sitting
room. 'Sit yourselves down, all you
relative people. I've just got one teensy-
tadpole-toenail-sized little thing to see to
in the kitchen, if you'd like to chat among
yourselves for a moment or two.'

Winnie leapt back into the kitchen and
started slamming plates down on the table.
Wilbur was busy mopping up tea. They
could overhear bits of conversation from
the room next door.

Uncle Owen said, 'Winnie will put me at the head of the table because I am the head of the family, being the oldest male here.'

'Ooer,' said Winnie. 'I'd better get that right.' She began to lay Uncle Owen's place at the head of the table.

'Oh, but I am older than you, Owen!' came Auntie Alice's voice. 'I always have been! Of course Winnie will put me at the head of the table!'

'Uh-oh!' muttered Winnie. 'Now, what do I do?'

Wilbur pointed to the other end.

'Good thinking, Wilbur!' said Winnie. 'A table has two ends!'

But now Cuthbert was complaining. 'I do have the highest magician degree among us, you know. I am the richest. So that makes me more important. Winnie will put . . .'

'. . . you all into highchairs for your tea,
if you're not careful!' said Winnie.
'Whatever shall I . . . Ooo, I've got an
idea, clever me! *Abracadabra!*'

And instantly she'd magicked a new
table.

'We're ready!' said Winnie, 'Oh, except
we still haven't got a teapot! Heck!
Where's the glue, Wilbur?'

As quick as she could, Winnie stuck
bits of teapot back into something like a
teapot shape. But she could hear her
guests talking again—

'Winnie will pour my cup of tea first,'
said Owen. 'She knows that I'm the most
important.'

'You're a knotty noodle, Owen!' said
Alice. 'Winnie will serve me first!'

'No, me of course!' said Cuthbert. 'Me,
me, me!'

'Silly things!' said Winnie. 'I'll soon
sort them! Where are those other pots,
Wilbur?'

At last Winnie was done, a bit gluey, a bit feathery, but ready for tea.

'Ahem,' she said as she went into the sitting room. 'Would you care to come through for tea now?'

Uncle Owen and Auntie Alice and Cousin Cuthbert all started pushing and pinching and . . .

'Behave yourselves!' said Winnie. 'You're all going to sit at the best place at the table . . . because the table is square!'

72

The relative people sat.

'Who would like tea?' asked Winnie.

'Me, me, me!' they all shouted (and not one of them said 'please').

'I shall pour you all the first cup of tea,' said Winnie. 'And I shall pour the first cup for myself as well.'

'Eh?' said the relative people as Winnie arranged four cups on the table. Then she took the cosy off her stuck-together pot, and she poured four cups of tea all at the same time.

'Oh!' said the relative people.

So everyone slurped and burped together and couldn't find much to quarrel about for the rest of teatime.

'Phew!' said Winnie as she closed the door on her guests. 'Let's have another cup, just the two of us this time, Wilbur.'

Winnie made a fresh pot of finest ditchwater tea.

'Mrrow!' warned Wilbur, but Winnie wasn't listening. She began to pour, and . . .

'A nice, hot tea footbath!' said Winnie, dabbling her toes. 'The perfect way to unwind after a busy day!'

75

Giddy-up,
WINNIE

'Come on, Dolly Drop!' shouted
Winnie, bouncing up and down on the
sofa and whacking it with her wand.
'Come on!'

She was watching horse racing on telly.

'Faster! Go on!'

Then a dreamy look came into Winnie's
eyes. 'Wouldn't it be wonderful to have a
horse and to go racing, Wilbur?'

'Mrrow!' Wilbur firmly shook his head.

Winnie's dreamy gaze wandered to her

wand, then to a rat on the floor. 'Wilbur, in *Cinderella* didn't they turn a rat into . . .? Ooo, yes!' Winnie waved her wand,

'**Abracadabra!**'

'Neeeeiiggghhh!'

Suddenly there was a horse standing where the rat had been. It was big and cloppy and clumsy. **Crash!** Things began to fall as the horse turned around. **Scrunch! Tinkle! Smash!** Winnie's furniture and knick-knacks went flying.

'Steady, boy!' said Winnie. 'Er . . . you don't look very much like a racing horse. And that's not hay, you great cloppy twit! That's my hair! Earwigs' elbows, where can I put a horse where it won't do any harm? I think the kitchen's the best place.'

78

Winnie filled the sink with water for the horse. She fed it carrots and sugar lumps.

Chomp! Chomp! 'Blooming heck, that didn't last long! You'll have to win me some prize money if you want to keep eating expensive sugar lumps!'

Winnie put a blanket over the horse.
She tied him to a table leg. 'Go to sleep
now,' she said. 'You and I are going racing
in the morning!'

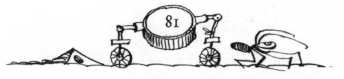

Winnie got into her nightie, and put her hair into a net. It did look a bit like black hay. Then she fell asleep, dreaming. 'Oh, thank you, your majesty,' she was telling the queen in her dream as she accepted a huge gold cup for winning the race. Then she was giving the horse a drink of champagne from the cup, and bubbles went up his nose and made him start to float, up and into the air, so Winnie caught hold of his tail and floated upwards too, and then ...

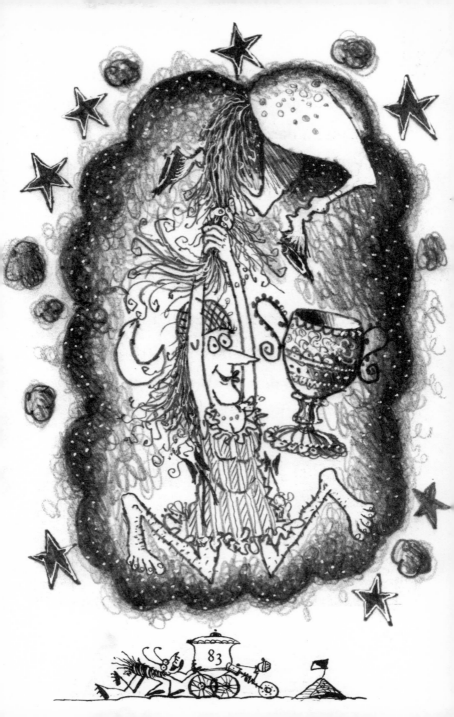

a horrible pong woke Winnie.

'Phewee! Hold your dose!' said Winnie, clutching her nose as they went into the kitchen.

'Neeeeiiggghhh!'

'Mrrow!'

There were piles of steaming horse poo all over the floor.

Winnie grabbed her broom and started
to sweep it up, but the broom sulked and
kicked and flicked. 'This bit of having a
horse is no fun,' said Winnie. 'But racing
it will be as fun as an iced sherbet bun.
Let's get going!'

Winnie put on jockeyish clothes, with her smallest cauldron on her head as a hat.

'Hey, Wilbur, we need a proper racing kind of name for our horse. They are always called something stupid, aren't they? How about Whinnying Wonder?'

'Mrrow.' Wilbur wasn't impressed.

'Or Wilbur and Winnie's Winning Wonder? We can call him Four Ws for short.'

'Meeeow!'

So Winnie wrote 'W W W W' on a corner of the horse blanket.

'Now he looks as smart as a snoreberry tart!' said Winnie. 'Help me get up onto Four Ws, Wilbur, and then off we go!'

'Oooer! It's very high up!' said Winnie when she was up. 'And he's as wide as a whale to sit on. Ooo, me legs!'

Winnie clicked her tongue. 'Gee-up!'
Nothing happened.

Winnie dangled a sugar lump from the
end of her wand and waved it in front of
Four Ws. Four Ws stretched his neck,
snatched the sugar lump and scrunched
the end of the wand, but he didn't move.
Winnie kicked with her heels. Winnie
whacked with her broken wand. 'Get
moving, you great useless thing!' Still
nothing happened . . . until Winnie's
broomstick decided to help. The
broomstick gave Four Ws a great whack
on the bottom. **WHUMPH!**

'Neeeeiiggghhh!'

Up reared Four Ws, and then he was
off, galloping with great clip-cloppy
hooves out of Winnie's house, down the
road towards the race track.

'I didn't think he'd be this fast!' said
Winnie.

89

They didn't get very far. Wilbur clung
on to Four Ws' tail for as long as he could,
but he fell when Four Ws jumped the
garden gate. Winnie lasted a little longer,
but she soon somersaulted off to land—
CLANG!—on her cauldron helmet, then
bounced into a ditch full of smelly, green
goo slime.

'Oh, toads' bottom warts!' said Winnie,
pulling pondy creatures from her hair.

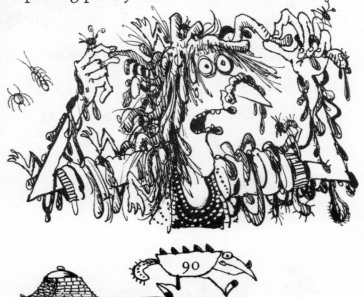

90

Winnie squelched sadly home to find
Wilbur busy stuffing mouse nests into the
foot of one of Winnie's pongy, holey old
socks.

'Whatever are you doing?' asked
Winnie, rubbing her bruises.

Wilbur pulled the sock over the top of Winnie's broomstick, and suddenly Winnie understood what he was doing. 'You're making a blooming hobby horse!' she said. 'Oo, you clever cat, you! More like a hobby zebra with those stripes!'

Winnie added half boiled-egg eyes and cabbage leaf ears to her broom hobby zebra horsey thing.

'Come on, Wilbur! If we're quick we can still make it for the last race!'

They hurried to the racetrack, hearing the cheers of the crowd and loudspeaker announcements as they got nearer—'The last race of the day is the all-comers' race. Horses to the paddock, please.'

'Quick!' said Winnie.

They joined the parade of horses and
jockeys around the ring. People pointed
and laughed at Winnie's horse.

'Take no notice!' said Winnie.

They lined up for the start. **Bang!**
And they were away! The proper horses
were galloping elegantly towards the first
jump with Winnie hobble-running
behind. Then she tripped and tumbled.

'Blasted bat bums!' said Winnie.

'Ha ha!' laughed the crowd.

'Abracadabra!' shouted Winnie.

Winnie's broomstick hobby zebra
horsey suddenly lifted Winnie and Wilbur
up, and charged fast after the galloping
horses. It swooped easily over the fence.
The broomstick hobby zebra horsey
turned and grinned his ghastly grin at the
horses coming up behind, and half of
them shied and swerved off-course.

'Giddy-up!' said Winnie, and on they
whizzed, before screeching to a halt over
the ditch, so all the other riders tried to
stop too and—**thump-bump!**—piled
into one another.

'Only one horse in front of us now!'
shouted Winnie. 'Come on, Broomy! I'll
never use you for sweeping horse poo
again if you win the race!'

The broomstick doubled its speed and
became a blur, winning the race by just
one smelly stuffed sock head's length.

'Hooray!' shouted Winnie.

'Hooray!' shouted the crowd.

'You can't have the winning cup,' said the snooty man in the hat. 'That's only for riders of real horses.'

'I don't mind,' said Winnie. 'I've got my own prize.' And she took something from her pocket, popped it into her mouth and began to scrunch. 'That's the best thing about a hobby horse.' She patted Broomy on the nose. 'You can eat the sugar lumps yourself!'

WINNIE'S
Fun Run

Crash! Winnie flung open the door and threw her shopping down.

'Wilbur, where are you? Wilburrrr?'

Wilbur was lying in a nice hot patch of sunshine on the floor behind the worm-noodle machine. He opened one eye, then closed it again.

'Wiiiiiillllbuuurrrr!' yelled Winnie.

Wilbur yawned a wide yawn. He stretched a wide stretch. Then he sighed.

'Wilbur!' Winnie pounced, grabbing

him and clutching him to her chest.
'Guess what, Wilbur?'

Wilbur raised an eyebrow.

'There's a fun run this afternoon, and it's fancy dress! With prizes!! Ooo, what shall I be, Wilbur? Something lovely-dovely beautiful-fruitiful!'

Wilbur rolled his eyes.

'Abracadabra!' went Winnie, and in an instant, there she was, dressed as a mermaid.

'I'll just get my comb from the
dressing-up table,' said Winnie.

But mermaids can't walk very well.
They are even worse at running.

Wobble-splat-crash!

'Blooming bloomers!' said Winnie,
rubbing her elbow. 'I need a fancy dress
outfit for somebody who uses legs a lot.
I know! *Abracadabra!*'

Instantly, Winnie became a ballerina,
twirling and swirling and twiddling and
twaddling on her tippy-toe tootsies
until ... **Crash!**

'Heck in a handbag!' said Winnie, rubbing her leg. 'That's no flipping good either!'

Wilbur put a claw to his chin and thought. Then he raised his claw in the air. 'Meeow!'

'What, Wilbur? What should I dress up as?'

Wilbur pointed to a picture on a wall of a handsome knight and a princess.

'That's it!' said Winnie. 'Abracadabra!'

And there stood Winnie in a suit of armour. **Clang! Wobble-clash crash!**

'Ouch!' said Winnie, rubbing her head. 'Er . . . or did you mean the girl one, Wilbur?'

'Meeeow!'

'Abracadabra!' Instantly Winnie was
dressed as a princess. Frills and flounces,
bows and bouncy bits, and all-over-pink.

'Oooo. I think I like this one!' said
Winnie. 'I'll be the prettiest one there,
don't you think, Wilbur?'

'Mmm,' said Wilbur.

'I'll win that big cup for the best costume, easy-peasy, elephant-with-a-cold sneezy! And I might even win the race cup too. Then I could put one at each end of the mantelpiece. I wonder if I can run in this dress?'

Winnie took a tentative step. Then another. She did a little jig. Then she ran around the room.

'This is brillaramaroodles for running in, but I must make sure I've got enough energy to run faster than everyone else. I need an energy drink.'

Winnie found a bottle of pond water and added some gnat's-pee cordial. 'But there's not much energy in those. Perhaps I can have some energy-boosting food.

Oo, I know what'll make me go fast!'
Winnie took down a jar from a top shelf.
She mixed cheetah claw clippings with
rocket-engine oil and ground them up to
make a smelly paste. Winnie held her
nose, and gulped down a big spoonful.

'Yuerk!' she said. 'Ooo, that is so very very very disgusting it must make a big difference!' And within moments it did make a difference. It made Winnie go very fast . . . to the loo!

When Winnie came out of the loo, she didn't look fit to run anywhere.

'I'm weak and wobbly!' wailed Winnie. 'Wilbur, however am I going to race?'

Wilbur helped Winnie down to the fun run field. Winnie tried warming up, running on the spot, knees hitting her chin, just for a moment. Then she collapsed and gasped for breath. 'Ooo, Wilbur, I'm as panty as a knicker factory! I can't run!' Then Winnie suddenly smiled. 'What if I had some trainers that would do the running for me? Am I a genius, Wilbur, or what?'

'Mrrrow,' said Wilbur.

'*Abradacabra!*' went Winnie, pointing her princessy pink wand at her princess shoes, and—zap!

Instantly her shoes turned into super
sporty speedy spongy sleeky stylish
trainers.

'On your marks!' said the race starter.
'Get set . . . GO!' And off ran everyone in
their costumes, all together . . . except for
Winnie, who was way out in front.

III

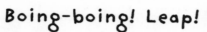

Boing-boing! Leap!

'Wow!' shouted Winnie. 'These are seven-league trainers! Watch me go!'

But Winnie's new trainers had a mind of their own. They veered Winnie off the track. They ran her dashing through hedges. Splashing through ditches. Thrashing through a haystack.

'Meeow!' called Wilbur as Winnie shrank into the distance. The left trainer must have been slightly stronger than the right one because Winnie was going round in a great big circle. Wilbur scratched his head, then, 'Mrroww!' he said. He had a plan. Wilbur found Jerry in the crowd, and he dragged him to stand with his arms out.

'Meeow, mrrrrrrow!' Wilbur told Scruff, so then Scruff knew what to do. Then they waited.

Meanwhile, Winnie was charging through the vegetable market. **Bang! Tumble! Squash! Splat!**

'Help!' **Pant pant!**

Winnie ran through the clothes market. **Rip! Tangle! Whoops! Sob, pant pant!**

But Winnie's trainers were running and running . . . back to where the race began. And there was Jerry with his arms out.

Oomph! Winnie ran slap bang into Jerry. Winnie's trainers were still running, but Jerry lifted Winnie off the ground. And then Scruff and Wilbur tackled a trainer each.

'Grrrr!'

'Hisss!'

They tugged and tussled those trainers off Winnie's feet, and they spat them out. Pah! Off ran the trainers, all on their own. They are probably running still.

So Winnie could wibbly-wobbly stand on her feet again, and not go anywhere.

'Oooo, I'm as shaky as a slug slime jelly. I never want to take another step!' she said. 'Fetch me a pushchair, would you?'

The fun runners were arriving back, and the winners were being announced by a crackly voice coming out of a loudspeaker. 'The winner of the best fancy dress costume is Winnie the Witch for her very convincing outfit and make-up!'

'Hooray!' shouted the crowd.

'Oh!' Winnie patted her hair. 'Well, I'm as surprised as a hair louse that wins a best pet award! Come with me to fetch the cup, Wilbur!'

Wilbur helped Winnie wobble up onto the stage to collect a huge twiddly trophy.

'There you are, madam,' said the man. 'Well deserved for your very impressive scarecrow outfit.'

'Scare—!' began an affronted Winnie. But Wilbur put a quick paw over her mouth and dragged her off the stage.

'Ah, well,' said Winnie as Jerry gave her a piggyback home. 'I'd rather be an impressive scarecrow than just one of a herd of pink princesses.'

'Meow,' agreed Wilbur.

WINNIE

Gets Bossy

Winnie sat with her dirty boots up on the fat-bellied armchair, spilling pop-corns and pop-bunions as she sat watching the telly.

Scratch-tug-tattify! Wilbur was happily scratching down the side of the same chair. His claws were ripping the fabric and tugging out the stuffing.

'See this?' said Winnie. 'That man's showing how you can make your room look interesting and new, just by moving

your furniture about a bit. Let's try it!'

Up jumped Winnie, spilling her fizzy
pickle-pop onto the chair seat. 'Let's
move the big table over to the window,'
said Winnie. Winnie pushed. 'Phew!
Come on, Wilbur, lend us a paw!'

So Wilbur pushed too. The table dug
its heels in.

Scrape-screech! Puff-pant!

went Winnie and Wilbur. The table was leaving lines of scrape marks.

'Oh, flipping fish flippers, look at that!' said Winnie. 'Pass me that rug, Wilbur.'

Wilbur and Winnie put the rug over the marks, but, **trip-smash!**

'That blooming rug tripped me on
purpose!' said Winnie. 'Humph!' Winnie
pulled out her wand. 'If all you pieces of
furniture think that you can behave as if
you're alive, then you might as well be
alive and blooming well move yourselves!
Most of you have got legs, so you can just
walk to where I want you!'

124

Winnie waved her wand.
'*Abracadabra!*'

Instantly the furniture sat up straight.

'Ooo, that's better!' said Winnie. 'Right
then, chairs, tuck in around the table. Go!'

Hup-two-three, the dining chairs
marched smartly into place, neatly under
the table.

'Brillaramaroodles!' said Winnie.
'Where's the elephant's earwax polish?'
Winnie put the tin of polish and one of her
old vests onto the table. 'Polish yourself,
please, table!' she said.

Up came one of the table's four legs to take hold of the polish tin. Up came another leg to take hold of the cloth. Then the table polished itself like a person brushing their hair.

'Oo, what else shall we make the furniture do?' said Winnie.

She went from room to room.

'Bed, make yourself!'

Winnie's bed did a kind of a jiggle and quiver, and all the bed covers fell into place, all neat and tight.

'Curtains, draw yourselves!'

Swish-swoosh!

'Ha haa! Do it again!' said Winnie.

Swish-swoosh!

'This is fun!'

Back downstairs, Winnie ordered,

'Chairs, do an Irish dance!'

The chairs shuffled out from under the table. They all lined up in a straight row. Their arms went down by their sides, then their legs began to prance and dance on the spot.

'Yay!' cheered Winnie. She and Wilbur joined in the dance. 'Hatstand, do a disco dance!'

And it did.

'Ha haa!' laughed Winnie. 'What next?'

Wilbur pointed at the fat-bellied armchair.

So Winnie told the fat-bellied armchair,
'Chair, dance a cha cha cha!'

The stumpy little legs of the fat-bellied
armchair tried to dance, but it wasn't good.

131

'Meee hee heeeow!' laughed Wilbur.

And suddenly there was a rumble grumble from all the furniture. The fat-bellied chair growled.

'Ooo, look!' said Winnie. The fat-bellied armchair was turning purple. It was puffing up and stamping its little legs and waving its fat little arms. Then it ran towards Wilbur.

132

'Hissss!' went Wilbur, then he was off and running too. Wilbur scrabbled up the dresser, and behind curtains that tried to wrap and trap him. Wilbur leapt onto the table, his claws skidding and screeching across the polished top, and—uh-oh!— the table flipped onto its back and grabbed Wilbur with all its legs as if it was a spider and Wilbur was a fly.

'Mrrrow!' wailed Wilbur.

'Ooo, Wilbur, the furniture is cross with you for all that scratching!' said Winnie.

But the furniture was cross with Winnie too. The fat-bellied chair came up fast behind the back of her legs, making her sit down in it very suddenly. The chair wrapped its fat padded arms around Winnie's waist.

'Ooo, help! Dining chairs, help me!' shouted Winnie. But those chairs all just crossed their arms. 'Cupboard?' said Winnie. The cupboard turned its back. 'Oh, pleeeeaase!' wailed Winnie. 'I promise I won't make you do anything you don't want to ever again!'

The fat-bellied chair let her go.

'Phew!'

The table let Wilbur free.

'Meeeow!'

But the stool marched over to the front door and opened it, **Crreeeeaaaakk!** Then the television, the bath, the bed, the chairs, the table, the hatstand, cupboards, and everything marched out of the door and away.

'They've left home!' wailed Winnie.

Winnie and Wilbur sat on the floor and ate their supper with fingers and paws because the cutlery in the dresser drawer had all gone with the dresser.

'We'll have to sleep on the floor with the cockroaches and ants,' said Winnie. 'It could be a tickly night!'

The floor was hard. The floor was draughty. The creepy crawlies did tickle.

Sigh! **Squirm.** 'Ouch!' **Hump.**

'Meeow!' **Scratch-itch!** Sigh!

Neither Winnie nor Wilbur could get to sleep.

'You know,' said Winnie, 'I liked our old furniture just the way it's always been. Oh, silly me!'

Then, suddenly, there was a **bang-bang-bang!** from the front door. **'Wiiinnniiieeee!'** yelled the dooryell.

'Ouch! Eeek!' Winnie got stiffly to her feet and walked stiffly to the door. 'I feel as if I'm made of blooming wood myself!' moaned Winnie.

Creeeeeak! She pulled the door
open. And in marched Winnie's bed, her
television, her table, her chairs, her bath . . .

'Hooo-blooming-ray!' said Winnie,
clapping her hands. 'Welcome home! Ooo,
here's my lovely favourite fat-bellied chair!'

'Hiss!' Wilbur leapt onto the windowsill.

'What brought you home, my furniture
friends?' asked Winnie.

The hatstand pointed outside. It was stormy and wet and cold and dark out there.

'Not nice,' agreed Winnie. 'Well, you all settle just wherever you want to be, and I'll magic you back to being your proper selves.

'Aaah!' sighed the furniture, each piece happily setting itself down. Some things ended up in rather odd places.

'Abracadabra!' went Winnie. And
everything went quiet.

'Meeeow?' asked Wilbur.

'Yes, it's safe to come down now,' said
Winnie. 'And we can go to bed in a proper
bed, even if that bed is in the kitchen. Oh,
blooming heck! Even if the bed is wet!
And rumpled! And full of leaves! Ouch!
And has a blooming hedgehog family
nesting in it!'

But Wilbur found something much
softer and drier and warmer to sleep on.
It was Winnie's stomach. He slumped to
saggy sleep with a smile. Then he worked
his claws as he purred.

'Ouch! Now I know how furniture
feels!' said Winnie. 'Put those blooming
claws away, Wilbur!'

Which is
WITCH?

Winnie was doing some shopping. She told the shopkeeper, 'I'd like six big gob sloppers please, and a sugar mouse for Wilbur.'

'That cat isn't allowed in this shop,' said the shopkeeper.

'What?' said Winnie. 'Why not? Wilbur goes everywhere with me.'

'He's not hygienic, that's why,' said the shopkeeper. 'Look at those paw prints!'

'Oo, I can soon sort that,' said Winnie.

'*Abracadabra!*'

'*Uh!*' gasped all the other customers, because Wilbur was suddenly floating just above the ground.

A man in a suit pointed at Winnie. 'Sh-she's a witch!' he said, and he ran out of the shop.

'Now look what you've done!' said the shopkeeper. 'You've lost me a customer!'

'Only one silly man,' said Winnie.
'Everyone in the village already knows
that I'm a witch.'

'I don't want you or your cat in my
shop again!' said the shopkeeper. 'I can't
be doing with complications! I just want
normal customers.'

'That's not fair!' said Winnie.

'Out!' said the shopkeeper.

Winnie and Wilbur pressed their faces up to the shop window to see all the things they couldn't buy because they weren't normal.

'The trouble is,' said Winnie, 'I don't know how to be *not a witch.*'

'Meeow,' agreed Wilbur.

'But maybe,' said Winnie, suddenly grinning as wide as a banana. 'Maybe we could learn how to be normal!'

'Meeow?'

'What we need is a normal person to come and stay at our house. Then we can study them and copy what they do.'

Winnie chose a dusty musty damp empty room for a normal person to live in. She waved her wand. 'Abradacabra!'

149

Instantly, there was a plump soft bed, nice spider-web curtains, and a vase of nettles on a bedside table. 'Lovely!' said Winnie.

'Purrr!' went Wilbur.

'Good. Now, can you make a sign, Wilbur?'

Wilbur dipped a claw into some paint, and he carefully wrote:

·WINNIE'S·
·Bed & Breakfast·
Comfy Bed · £13 · Yummy Food
PLUS 13% VAT
·NORMAL LADIES ONLY·

They stuck the sign in place. Then they waited. And waited.

'Do you think it's the price that's putting them off?' asked Winnie. So Wilbur wrote 'FREE' in big letters over the sign.

Then they waited again, and waited some more. 'Perhaps they've all heard that I'm a witch, and they don't like witches?' said Winnie.

'**Brriiiinnngg! Wiiiinnniiieee!**'
went the dooryell.

'Hooray! Somebody's come!' shouted
Winnie.

Crreeeaaaak! Winnie opened the door.
There stood a serious looking lady. 'I've come
for bed and breakfast,' said the lady.

'Oh, goody!' said Winnie. 'Er . . . excuse
me asking, but are you normal?'

'Yes, I think so!' said the lady.

'Brillaramaroodles!' said Winnie. 'What's
your name?'

'I am Dr Which,' said the lady.

'Really?!' said Winnie, clapping her hands
together. 'That's a funny thing because
I'm a . . . Ooo!' Winnie slapped a hand
over her mouth.

152

'That's quite all right,' said Dr Which.
'In fact you being a witch is the reason
I am here. I am simply fascinated by
witches. I intend to study you. You don't
mind, do you?'

'That's as perfect as if baby slugs were
born already coated in chocolate, that is!
Because I want to study you too!'

'Well, that's marvellous,' said Dr
Which.

'Oh,' said Dr Which when she saw the
bedroom. She scribbled notes. 'Fascinating!'
she said. 'Fascinating!'

'What is?' asked Winnie.

'Simply everything about you!' said
Dr Which.

'Oh, dear,' said Winnie. 'Because I'm
not fascinated by you yet.'

Winnie served a lovely alligator-egg
soufflé for supper.

'How marvellously fascinating!' said Dr
Which, and she made notes, but she didn't
eat the soufflé. She spent the whole
evening just looking at Winnie and
looking at Winnie's house and looking at
Wilbur. She scribbled lots of notes.
'Fascinating!' was all she said.

Normal people are a bit boring, was what
Winnie thought. She went to bed early.

In the morning Dr Which asked,
'Winnie, is there a shop nearby? I'd like to
buy myself some normal food.'

'Don't you like my food?' said Winnie.
'Oo, I know! Let's swap clothes and go
to the shop that way!'

157

'Why?' asked Dr Which.

'So that you can feel what it's like being a witch,' said Winnie. 'And I can look normal and buy some gob sloppers.'

'What a marvellously fascinating idea!' said Dr Which.

Wilbur had to go with Dr Which. 'Mrrrow!' he complained.

'I'll get you lots of sugar mice!' promised Winnie.

Dr Which and Wilbur went into the shop. 'A normal cheese sandwich, please,' said Dr Which.

The shopkeeper held up a hand. 'Oh, no you don't!' he said. 'Out you go! You and your cat! No witches in here!'

'Fascinating!' said Dr Which.

'Out!' said the shopkeeper.

So out she went. And in came Winnie.

'Good morning, madam!' said the shopkeeper. 'And how may I help you?'

'You can give me a large bag of gob sloppers, that's how,' said Winnie. 'And a bag of sugar mice.'

'Gob sloppers? Sugar mice?' The shopkeeper peered closely at Winnie. Winnie glared back through Dr Which's glasses. 'Er . . . yes, at once,' he said.

As the shopkeeper was opening the jar
of sugar mice, Mrs Parmar came into the
shop with her shopping bag on wheels,
and **whoops!** one of the wheels caught
a box that shifted a display that toppled
onto a table that flipped like a seesaw to
shower fruit and vegetables everywhere.

Bop! Splat! Ping-ping! Boing!

'Ow, get off!' said the customers as they were pinged and splatted.

'You'll have to pay for cleaning this shirt, Mr Shopkeeper!'

'And for my black eye!'

'Oh, dear!' said Mrs Parmar.

'Oh, no!' said the shopkeeper. Mice came scurrying out of every nook and cranny, scrabbling for the food. It was CHAOS!

'Fetch our friend Winnie the Witch!'
said a customer. 'Her magic could save us!'

'Actually!' said Winnie, stepping
forward and taking off Dr Which's glasses.
'I am Winnie, Winnie the Witch.'
   'Hooray!'

'But I'm not allowed to do magic in the shop because it's not normal,' said Winnie.

Splat! Squeak! Mice were running up the shopkeeper's trouser legs.

'Oh, please do your magic, Winnie!' he pleaded.

So Winnie pulled out her wand. She waved it, *'Abracadabra!'*

Instantly everything jumped back into place . . . except for a couple of mice who sat and smirked at the shopkeeper.

'I d-d-don't like mice!' he said.

'Would you like a cat to catch them?' asked Winnie. 'Wilbur! In you come!'

Ting! Pounce! Squeak!

So Wilbur had normal mice as well as sugar mice for his tea.

WINNIE

on Patrol

'Almost home, Wilbur!' said Winnie, steering her broomstick over the dusky wood.

'Twoooo!' called a cross owl.

Swerve! 'Whoops!' said Winnie.

'Meeeow!' Wilbur's fur was on end.

'You're right, Wilbur,' said Winnie. 'That owl should have lights! Let's fly up the village street. It'll be safer there.'

They swooped along the main road through the village, then, **Bang! Crash!**

Crunch! Tinkle! Winnie's broom hit Mrs Parmar's bike. Bike, witch, cat, broom and school secretary all fell **clatter-crump!** into the road.

'Ouch, my bum!' said Winnie.

'Mrrrow!' went Wilbur.

'That's really dangerous!' said Mrs Parmar, standing up and wagging a finger at Winnie. 'What if I had been a lorry instead of a bike?'

'I didn't see you!' said Winnie.

Mrs Parmar put her hands on her hips. 'Where, Winnie the Witch, were your broom lights?'

'What lights?' said Winnie.

'Precisely!' said Mrs Parmar. 'You haven't got any! And everybody knows that a road user must have lights on their vehicle. It says so in the law.'

'Where are your lights, then?' asked Winnie.

'Here and here!' said Mrs Parmar, pointing. 'Oh. Er . . . the batteries seem to have run out. But at least I do have lights!'

169

They got safely onto the pavement, just as a glare of bright lights came fast around the corner.

Vrooom! The car whizzed past them.

'Coo-er,' said Winnie.

Gulp! went Mrs Parmar.

Wilbur's fur stood on end.

'We need to do something about this!' said Winnie. **'Abracadabra!'**

Instantly, Winnie's broom and Mrs Parmar's bike were strung with fairy lights. Mrs Parmar had a flashing light on her backside, and another two on the back of each hand. Wilbur had a light on the end of his tail. He thrashed it crossly. And Winnie had a winking light on the top of her hat.

'That's better!' said Winnie. 'Goodbye, Mrs Parmar.'

'Goodbye, Winnie. Ouch!' said Mrs Parmar as she tried to sit on her bike and found that a light wasn't a comfortable thing to sit on.

Back home, drinking mugs of cocoa, Winnie was frowning and stroking her chin.

'Hmmm,' she said.

'Meeow?' asked Wilbur.

'I'm just thinking about those little ordinaries,' said Winnie. 'In the winter it's dark by the time they come out of school. I think they all need flashing lights too . . .'

Brriiing-trrriiing-zzziiinngg!

went Winnie's telling-moan.

'Whoever . . .?' said Winnie. It was Mrs Parmar. 'Oh, yes?' said Winnie. 'I see . . . yes . . . you're quite right . . . well, yes . . . bye!'

'Meeow?' asked Wilbur.

'Guess what?' said Winnie. 'Mrs Parmar wants the little ordinaries to be safe too. She's asked me to be their Crossing Patrol Supervisor! With a uniform and everything! I'll look as smart as a jam tart!'

173

Next morning, Winnie and Wilbur reported to the school office.

'Is it a pretty uniform?' asked Winnie.

Mrs Parmar handed Winnie a great big long bright yellow coat, and a matching cap.

'They're a bit big!' said Winnie.

'Everybody will see you,' said Mrs Parmar. 'Now, here's the sign that you'll use to stop the cars.' She handed Winnie a big stick with stripes down it.

'Just like my tights!' said Winnie.

On one side it had a big red circle with a picture of children and on the other side there was a word.

'What does that say?' asked Winnie.

'It says "STOP",' said Mrs Parmar.

'Do you think they will?' said Winnie.

They went out to the road.

'What we really need is one of those black and white stripy things across the road,' said Mrs Parmar.

'Easy peasy!' said Winnie. She waved her wand. 'Abracadabra!'

And there was a zebra running across the road.

Beeep! Screeech! Shout-shout!

'It doesn't work very well,' said Winnie.

'We don't want a zebra!' said Mrs Parmar, her chins all wobbling. 'Don't you know anything about the Highway Code?' she shouted as a noisy lorry rumbled past.

'Did you say a Highway Toad?' asked Winnie. 'I can get one of those. *Abracadabra!*'

And suddenly there was a toad in a motor car, buzzing back and forth through the traffic.

'No, no, no!' said Mrs Parmar. 'Dear, oh, dear!'

Vroom-beep-beep!

'I don't think your ideas are very good, Mrs P,' said Winnie.

Mrs Parmar looked at Winnie. 'Just use your lollipop,' she said.

Children were waiting to cross the road. They told Winnie, 'Watch for a gap in the traffic. Then hold up your lollipop and walk into the road and the cars will stop.'

'Okey-dokey,' said Winnie. She waited
for a gap. She held out her stick, and she
stepped out into the road.

Vroom-stop! went the cars.

'Good cars,' said Winnie. She stood
with her arms out like a scarecrow and the
children all walked safely across the road.

'Brillaramaroodles!' said Winnie, and she stepped back onto the pavement. 'It worked! Easy-peasy squashed worm squeezy!'

'Well done!' said the children.

'Er . . .' said Winnie, 'did you call my sign a lollipop?'

'Everyone calls them lollipops because that's what they look like!' said the children.

'Cooer!' said Winnie. 'It's a blooming big lollipop, isn't it?' Winnie stuck out her tongue. She gave her lollipop a great big lick. Then she made a face. **Spit!** **Euuggghh!** 'Horrible! Still, we can soon change that. *Abracadabra!*'

The STOP sign was instantly turned into shiny sticky sugary candy, raspberry flavoured in the red bits, lemon flavoured in the yellow bits, liquorice flavoured in the black bits.

'Mmmm, much nicer!' said Winnie.

The children jumped around her.

'Can I have a lick?'

'Please, Winnie, let me!'

But Mrs Parmar held up her hand

'Sharing lollipops is not hygienic!' she said.

'I'll give them a little lollipop each, then,' said Winnie. 'Everybody close your eyes and think of your favourite flavour. *Abracadabra!*'

Next moment, everyone had a lollipop. Even Mrs Parmar (her lollipop was flavoured with Brussels sprouts in gravy), even Wilbur (whose lollipop tasted of pilchards), even the car drivers.

'Mnn, that's all very well!' said Mrs
Parmar, trying to sound cross but not
being able to resist just one lick, and then
another. 'But how am I going to get these
children into school while you are offering
them sweets out here?' Lick!

'Oh, sorry!' said Winnie. 'How about if
... *Abracadabra!*'

185

Suddenly the school was made of gingerbread walls, with barley sugar door handles and chocolate biscuit roof slates.

'Wow!' said the children, and they all rushed towards school faster than they ever had before.

'Er . . . thank you, Winnie. I think,' said Mrs Parmar, and she followed the children inside.

'They'll need us again at going-home
time,' said Winnie to Wilbur. 'It'll be dark
then. I think I'll give all the little ordinaries
bells to wear so that everyone hears them
coming. And lights so we can see them.
Perhaps smells too?'

Winnie and Wilbur trotted home on the
zebra, sucking lollipops and thinking up
lots more safety ideas. The toad drove
off on his own adventures.

WINNIE'S
Perfect Pet

Wilbur was lying in the sun on the front
doorstep, slumped in the sunshine, when
Winnie came rushing over.

'Wilbur!' she said. 'Oh, Wilbur, there's
a huge man as big as a ginormous giraffe
moved in next door! And he's as rude as a
bee's fluffy bottom! He called me a scruff!'

Wilbur opened one eye. He looked at
Winnie, then he closed the eye again.

'Play with me, Wilbur,' said Winnie.

'Take my mind off that rude man. That's what a good pet would do.'

Wilbur yawned. He got up slowly, arched his back high, stretched his legs long, then sagged back into snoozing.

'You're as lazy as a hot lizard full of lunch!' said Winnie. 'Come on, let's play tennis, Wilbur!'

Winnie rushed indoors. She crashed
through the kitchen. She bumped through
the battery. She wriggled through the
wormery. She skipped through the spidery.
Then she came to the hall where she tugged
open the door under the stairs, and out
fell . . . everything!

'There it is!'

191

Winnie pounced. First, she tugged at something grey and tatty. Then she pulled out something that looked like a big holey spoon, and something else that looked like a mouldy old orange. She nipped into the loo . . . and came out looking like . . . um . . . this!

Winnie skipped, wriggled, bumped, and crashed back outside.

'What d'you think, Wilbur?'

Wilbur just put his paws over his face.

Winnie bounced the ball all around Wilbur. **Bounce, bounce.** 'Come on,' she said. 'Time to play!'

Wilbur didn't move.

'You're no fun,' said Winnie. 'I'll play with magic, if you won't play.'

Winnie pointed her wand at the racket and ball. '*Abracadabra, abracadabra, abracadabra!*' she shouted.

In an instant there were three tennis rackets and three more balls, all in the air. The rackets were hitting balls at Winnie.

Winnie waved her own racket, up
'Hup!', down **'Ooph!'**, around **'Aah!'**,
but she missed every ball.

'Ow! Ouch! Get off! Stop!' she shouted.
'Gnats' knickers!' she said. 'Nobody's nice
to me today, not even my wand!'

Winnie picked up her wand and she
threw it far into the undergrowth but,
a moment later, the wand was back . . .
in the mouth of a dog.

The dog came bounding up to Winnie.
It dropped the wand at Winnie's feet, then
grinned up at her and wagged its tail.

'Who are you?' said Winnie. 'Do you
want me to throw it again?'

Winnie threw the wand again, and
again, and again. And each time the dog
brought it back and wagged for more.
Winnie threw the ball too.

'Fetch!'

Back came the dog with the ball.

'Clever boy! Did you see that, Wilbur?
Isn't he a clever dog?'

'Mreow,' said Wilbur.

'Don't you like him?' said Winnie.

'I do. I like him ever so much. Let's all
have lunch together.'

So they went into the kitchen. Wilbur
nudged the dog. Wilbur winked at the
dog. Wilbur pointed at a packet of kipper
biscuits. Wilbur nodded in the direction
of Winnie. The dog grinned and nodded
his head and wagged his tail. He took the
biscuit box in his mouth and he presented
it to Winnie.

'For me?' said Winnie, not really
looking. 'Oh, isn't he a good dog, Wilbur?'
Winnie dipped a hand into the box, then
popped a biscuit into her mouth.

'Euch! Pah!' spat Winnie. 'Yuck!
Horrible, horrible! Kipper biscuits, I hate
'em!' She danced around, making faces and
waggling her tongue.

The dog hid under the table.

Wilbur puffed out his chest and grinned. Then he prepared a tray with Winnie's really favourite lunch snacks. Crispy worms. A nettle sandwich. A cup of slug smoothie.

'Yummy!' said Winnie. 'You're the *really* clever boy, Wilbur. You know just what I like!'

But the dog stuck out a leg and . . .

Trip! went Wilbur. **Crash!** went the tray.

Splat! went the smoothie, while crispy worms rained down on Winnie.

'Oh, Wilbur, you're as clumsy as a centipede on skates!' shouted Winnie.

Wilbur and the dog were busy sticking tongues out at each other. But, 'I've just had a brillaramaroodle idea!' said Winnie, perking up. 'Can you two guess what it is?'

The dog and Wilbur both shook their heads. 'It's obvious!' said Winnie. 'Cats are clever and dogs are obedient. I want a pet that's both of those things, so what I need is a *cog*!'

'Yowl!' went the dog.

'Mrrreow!' went Wilbur.

They both raced for the door, but Winnie was already stirring with her wand. *'Abracadabra!'*

Magic whirled and swirled, and in an instant there was . . . a cog.

'Perfect,' said Winnie.

But the cog was not perfect. It bounded up the curtains and chewed them to bits.

'MEEEEOW-WOOF!' Chew-chew, munch.

203

Winnie reached out a hand. 'Good cog,' she said.

But the cog hissed at her. Then it lifted its leg and weed on her foot.

'Euch! Bad cog!' said Winnie.

The cog jumped onto the sink, then out of the window into the garden. It began to dig.

'Come back!' shouted Winnie.

The cog took no notice. It dug a big muddy hole. It rolled in the mud. Then it sat and lifted a leg and licked the mud off it. It sniffed Winnie's bottom, then it jumped up at Winnie with muddy paws and scratchy claws.

'Get down!' said Winnie. 'Sit! Naughty boy! Wilbur, save me!'

But of course Wilbur wasn't there. Oh, dear, thought Winnie. This cog isn't the best bits of a dog mixed with the best bits of a cat after all. It's the worst of both of them joined together!

'Where's my wand? I want my Wilbur back.'

Winnie saw the wand on the ground. The cog saw it too, and it began to run towards the wand, its teeth snip-snapping.

'It's *my* wand!' shouted Winnie as she leapt into a magnificent dive, up and over and down, to grab the wand, and waved it—'Abracadabra!'—just as the cog's teeth were about to snap it in two.

Then there was Wilbur, looking shocked but pleased. And there was the dog, running away down the drive.

'Scruff!' boomed a big voice.

Winnie put her hands on her hips. 'It's that rude man again,' she said. 'He's as rude as ten frogs' bottoms, he is!'

But the dog was jumping around the man, wagging its tail and woofing.

'Scruffy, my dear old Scruff!' laughed the man.

Then Winnie smiled. 'Know what,
Wilbur?' she said. 'It's the dog that's a
Scruff, not me! There's nothing wrong
with me after all. And nothing wrong with
you either, come to that. Give us a kiss,
Wilbur!'

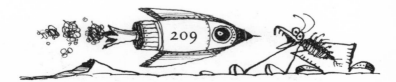

209

WINNIE
Fixes It

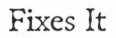

'See this, Wilbur?' asked Winnie. She was waving *Witch One?* magazine under his nose. 'I want one of those conservatory things.'

Wilbur did a squint.

'What do I want it for?' said Winnie. 'For growing plants in, that's what. Just think, Wilbur, we could have our own jungle with creepers and vines. We could keep exotic insects in it!' Winnie licked

her lips. 'Oo, it makes me hungry just thinking about it! Right,' said Winnie. 'Stand back!' She pointed her wand at the picture.

'*Abracadabra!*'

In an instant, there stood a beautiful shiny glass conservatory. But, 'Oh, soggy babies' bottoms,' said Winnie.

The conservatory was perfect in every way . . . except for its size. It was the same size as the picture. 'I'll use it for keeping my toenail clippings in,' said Winnie, putting it on the table. 'Let's try again. Get it BIG this time, wand!' Winnie whacked the wand hard on the page.

'Abracadabra!'

Instantly Winnie and Wilbur were
fighting something huge that flapped
down on them from above.

'I can't see!' said Winnie. 'The sky has
fallen! Where are you, Wilbur?'

Wilbur fought and spat and clawed and
scratched and bit . . . and escaped from
the giant magazine page. He hauled
Winnie out from under it.

'Oh, nits' knickers!' said Winnie.
'Magic isn't going to work for this.'

Wilbur began to build a tower with bits of earwigs' earwax fudge.

'That's it, Wilbur!' said Winnie. 'Clever boy! We'll get a proper builder in to build us a conservatory, just like normal people do. Do we know a builder?'

Wilbur did.

'What?' said Winnie. 'That great big man from next door? Are you sure?'

Wilbur was right. There was a new sign up. 'Build Your Dreams with Jerry the Builder.'

'He's already done some work on his own house,' said Winnie. 'Look!'

Jerry had had to lift the roof and extend the doors of his house because Jerry was a giant.

'A big chap like that should be able to build things almost as fast as magic,' said Winnie. 'Shall we ask him if he's free?'

217

'People from the village, they sees my sign and they knocks on the door,' said Jerry, scratching his head. 'But they always runs away when I opens it. So I'm vacant at the moment, missus.'

So Jerry came with his dog and his bag
of tools and his radio, and he set to work.
But a big chap like Jerry didn't fit into
Winnie's house very comfortably.

BEND, BUMP!

'Ouch!'

CRASH, BANG!

'Oooch!'

'Better build from the outside,' said Winnie.

But, 'Got to make a hole for where the conservatory will join the house,' said Jerry. 'Stand back, missus!' Jerry swung back a huge great mallet, then—**THUNK!**—he hit the wall. **CRASH!** Bricks tumbled, tiles tumbled, windows tumbled.

'Oh, no!' said Winnie.

A whole turret tumbled.

'Whoops!' said Jerry. 'Sorry, missus!'

Winnie's house was opened up like a doll's house. You could see all her bits and pieces, and Wilbur's too.

'That's not safe to go into now,' said Jerry. 'Not till I've put some beaming support whatnots in.' Jerry looked at his fob watch. 'It's time for me to finish for the day now. I'll see you tomorrow, missus.'

'Hang on a blooming mini-minute!' said Winnie, but Jerry had picked up his bag and was on his way.

'Well,' said Winnie, hands on hips.
'We'll just have to sleep in the garden like
snails tonight.'

Winnie and Wilbur put a sleeping bag
on the lawn.

'Eeek!' wailed Winnie. 'This grass is
wet! We need a floor, Wilbur.'

So Winnie and Wilbur went to Jerry's building yard. They dragged back some planks, laid them down, and fixed them together. They put the sleeping bag onto their new floor.

'That's better,' said Winnie, snuggling into the bag.

'Yip yip!' came a noise from the woods.

'Snarl!'

'Hisss!'

'Howl!'

'Yip yip yip!'

Winnie sat up, with her hair on end.

'What the heck was that? Wilbur?'

Wilbur had buried himself deep in the
sleeping bag.

'This is no blooming good,' said Winnie.

'We need some walls to keep us safe!'

So Winnie and Wilbur went back to Jerry's yard where they found some old windows. They fixed them up to make a wall.

'That's better!' said Winnie, snuggling down in the bag. 'Look at those stars, Wilbur! They're as beautiful as dandruff on velvet.'

Wilbur yawned. *Snore-purr.*

'We should sleep out here more often, Wilbur,' said Winnie.

Splat!

'What . . .?' began Winnie.

Split-splot!

'Mrrow!' Wilbur woke with a start. He'd suddenly turned into a black and white cat.

'He hee, look at you!' laughed Winnie. 'You look like a cow! Or a magpie!'

But then Winnie looked at herself. 'Oooo, yucky-horrible owls! We need a roof, that's what we need, Wilbur!'

So Winnie and Wilbur collected all the bits of broken glass that had fallen when Jerry made his hole.

'We just need some sticky-icky spider spit glue.' Winnie waved her wand over the broken glass. *Abracadabra!*

And instantly the bits of glass were joined together into a crazy kind of glass roof.

'That's fixed it!' said Winnie, snuggling
down into the sleeping bag. Then she
squinted. 'What the fish-toed heck is that?'

It was the sun, just beginning to come up.

'Oh, blooming blasted heck!' said Winnie,
reaching for her wand again.

'Abracadabra!'

Instantly there were plants in pots,
sheltering Winnie and Wilbur from the light.

Winnie and Wilbur slept at last, until . .

. **THUMP THUMP** . . . footsteps woke
them.

'Mornin', missus,' said Jerry, knocking
on the glass. 'Gor, you've gone and
built your own conservatory!'

'Have I?' said Winnie. 'But what a
blooming mess! Where's my wand?
Abracadabra!'

And instantly Winnie's conservatory
smartened up and fixed itself to the house.
Jerry scratched his head.

'Now I'm vacant again, with
nuffink to do. Bovver.'

They went to find out. The school in
the village looked a bit like Winnie's
house. But there were children running
around in a playground and shouting.

'Look, Wilbur!' said Winnie. 'Lots of
little ordinaries! Ring the doorbell.'

237

But the school secretary didn't want
Winnie in her school. Mrs Parmar was big
and scary, and so was her smile.

'This is a school for children, not for
grown-up witches,' she said. 'Off you go!'

238

'As a matter of fact, there is,' said the lady. 'Can you cook?'

'Can I cook? Are slugs slimy? Yes,' said Winnie. 'I'm ever so good at cooking.' She looked at the mice dangling in Wilbur's mouth. 'In fact I could use—'

But Wilbur slammed a paw over Winnie's mouth to stop her from finishing what she was going to say.

The lady gave Winnie the proper
clothes and hat to wear for cooking.

'I've got to go now,' said the lady. 'But
it's spaghetti bolognaise and ratatouille on
the menu today. Good luck!' And off she
went.

'Right,' said Winnie. 'Where do they
keep the cauldrons? Let's get cooking.
Ratatouille sounds yummy-scrummy.
Look in the fridge, Wilbur, and bring out
the rats.'

242

Wilbur looked in the fridge and in the larder. There were sacks of onions and boxes of aubergines and red and yellow peppers and courgettes, but no rats anywhere.

'Aha, I bet I know why,' said Winnie. 'They like things as fresh as possible for school dinners these days. You'll just have to catch the rats now, Wilbur. Quick as you can!'

Wilbur raced out of the door and into the sheds by the school field. *Leap, screech, wallop!* That was one rat caught. *Sneak, pounce, squeal!* That was another.

Meanwhile Winnie had remembered that the cook had said something about bolognaise.

'I do a lovely worm bolognaise,' said
Winnie. 'I suppose those worms will have
to be caught fresh as well.'

Off she went to the football pitch
where she waved her wand.

'Abracadabra!'

Instantly, worms wriggled up from the
ground and Winnie picked and pulled
them and chucked them into a bucket.

245

Before long, Winnie and Wilbur were
back in the kitchen, cooking as fast as
they could.

Clang-clang!

'Dinner time already! Quick, Wilbur,
put on a clean pinny and get ready to serve!'

Winnie heaved the cauldron onto the
counter just as the children started to come
through the door.

But somebody large was pushing to the front of the queue.

'Out of the way, children! Have some respect! Adults first!'

It was Mrs Parmar, pushing to the front. She thrust her tray towards Winnie. 'I'll have a large helping of that!' she said, pointing a fat finger at the cauldron.

Winnie ladled out wriggling worm bolognaise.

'This food is moving!' said Mrs Parmar.

'Just goes to show that it's really fresh,' said Winnie.

'In that case I'll have more of it!' said Mrs Parmar.

'Greedy pig!' said Winnie, but she ladled out more.

'And I'll have those novelty shape things too!' said Mrs Parmar, pointing at Wilbur's rats. 'I'll have three of those!'

Mrs Parmar sat down at a table and started to raise a forkful of worm bolognaise into her mouth. But a moment later she was shrieking.

'Euch!' *Spit!* 'Absolutely disgusting!'

Mrs Parmar was leaping around the place.

'You've poisoned me! Yeuch! What in the world have you fed me?'

'Ratatouille,' said Winnie. 'Made with lovely fresh rats. And bolognaise with freshly harvested worms. What's your problem?'

Mrs Parmar ran out of the hall.

But then Winnie noticed that it wasn't only Mrs Parmar who had a problem with the food. All the children were backing away from the serving hatch, hurrying to get out of the hall.

'Don't go, you little ordinaries!' called
Winnie. 'Have your lunch!'

'But we don't want to eat worms and
rats,' said a boy.

'Really?' said Winnie. 'How strange!
Well, that's easily solved. What would you
really like to eat, little boy?'

'Doughnuts!'

'Ice cream!'

'Easy-peasy lemon squeezy!' said
Winnie. She took out her wand and she
waved it over the food.

'Abracadabra!'

And instantly the rats and the worms were replaced by plates and plates of lovely party food.

'Yum!' shouted all the children, and they all ate lots. Winnie sat and ate and chatted with them. Wilbur showed off on the climbing equipment around the hall, while the children cheered him on.

252

Until Mrs Parmar came back in.

'Back to your classrooms, everyone!'

She waved a fat finger at Winnie.

'As for you!' said Mrs Parmar, her chins all wobbling. 'Clear away all this mess, and then go!'

'What about tomorrow?' asked Winnie. 'I thought I might do hot dogs.'

'Go!' said Mrs Parmar.

The clearing up was easy.

'Abracadabra!'

Instantly the kitchen was clean and tidy.

Then Winnie and Wilbur went home to their own dirty messy homely kitchen to cook their own tea.

'Ah, well,' sighed Winnie. 'At least there's one thing I learnt at school today.'

'Mrrow?' asked Wilbur.

'I've learnt a new letter,' said Winnie. 'Try this one, Wilbur. I spy with my little eye something beginning with "Q".'

Wilbur frowned. Wilbur looked around. Wilbur pointed.

'No!' said Winnie. 'Not a "quill". No, not a "quail" either. Nor the "Queen". D'you give up?'

Wilbur nodded.

'It's cucumber!'

'Mrrow!'

'What do you mean, cucumber doesn't begin with "Q"?' said Winnie. 'Listen to it . . . *cu*cumber!'

Wilbur sunk his head into his paws.

WINNIE
the Twit

'How many—' *slurp munch* '—have you got in your bucket, Wilbur?' asked Winnie.

They were picking dew-fresh caterpillars off pongberry trees.

Wilbur showed his bucket of wriggling, hairy, stripy caterpillars.

'Oo, well done, Wilbur! Yummy!' said Winnie. She opened her mouth wide, like a baby bird, and threw a caterpillar in. 'Mmn. I should stop eating them or there won't be

enough to make the jam. But they are so delicious, freshly picked!' Winnie poked a finger into her mouth to pick the bits of caterpillar stuck to her teeth. *Burp!* 'Isn't nature wonderful, Wilbur? It gives us everything we need.'

Wilbur sniffed a caterpillar, and sneezed. Tentatively, he nibbled a tiny bit of hairy caterpillar bottom.

'Meeeuch!' He spat it out!

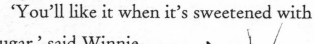

'You'll like it when it's sweetened with sugar,' said Winnie.

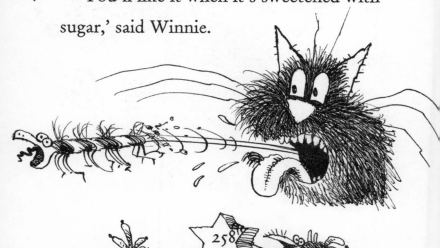

258

Wilbur sighed and thought longingly of
tinned tripe seasoned with fleas. He
thought of snail slime lollies from the deep
freeze. Wilbur sat down dreamily . . .
straight onto a patch of stinging nettles.

'Meeeeooooww! Hissss!'

'You should pick them, not sit on them!'
said Winnie. 'They make a lovely soup.'

'Ooo, look, a toad!' said Winnie, parting the long grass. 'There he goes!' Winnie dived like a goalkeeper . . . **weeeeooooww** . . . and caught the toad mid-hop.

'Ribbit!' said the toad.

'Got him!' shouted Winnie. 'We'll have Toad-in-the-Hole for lunch!'

'Ribbit!' went the toad, and it hopped on to Winnie's head and away.

'Quick, chase him!' shouted Winnie,
but Wilbur raised an eyebrow.

'Oh, all right,' said Winnie. 'We'll just
have Hole for lunch. Hole with nettle
sauce. Then we'll make that jam.'

Most of the day was spent in the steamy
kitchen, stirring cauldrons full of sticky
caterpillar jam.

'Tip in more sugar, Wilbur!' said
Winnie. She dipped in her wand and gave
it a lick. 'Eeeek! Ouch! Too hot!'

She waved the wand to cool the jam,
then licked again.

'Delicioso! Have a taste, Wilbur.'

Then suddenly Winnie went green. She
clutched her tummy.

'Um,' she said. 'I think I've maybe had
enough caterpillars for the moment.' She
did a big burp. 'Actually, Wilbur, I think
I'll just go outside for a bit of air.'

Winnie wandered out, and the beautiful
red sun and pink sky behind upside-down
broomstick trees soon made her forget her
tummy.

'Absolutely blooming beeeeautiful!'
sighed Winnie. 'Oo, did I hear
something?'

'Twoo twit!'

'Snails in the sweet jar! Whatever was
that?' Winnie's voice quivered. 'That
sounded like an owl, but different
somehow.'

'Twoo twit!'

'It must be a new kind of owl!
Something rare, perhaps. Ooo, I must
peek a look at it, and then I can tell
Wilbur all about what he's missed!'

Winnie went tiptoeing into the wood.

'Twooo twit! Twoooo twit!' she called.

Winnie listened. There was no sound
except the buzzing of evening midges.

'Has it flown away?' Winnie tried again.

'Twooo twit! Twooo twit! Twoooo twit!'
And this time . . .

'Twoooo twit!' came a reply.

'Oh, oh!' went Winnie. She could hardly
believe it! 'Twooo twit!' Winnie's eyes were
darting here and there amongst the dark
trees, looking for the owl. 'Twooo twit!'
she called.

'Twooo twit!'

'Where are you, owly?' whispered Winnie,
her hands clasped together. She waded
through the tangle of plants, pushing them
aside like a swimmer.

'Twooo twit!'

'Twooo twit!'

. . . And, **BUMP!** Winnie walked straight into something big and soft, and she bounced off it and landed on her bum.

'Knotted nanny goats! What the heck kind of an owl can it be?'

'Is you all right, missus?' asked a voice from above. It was Jerry, the giant from next door.

'Jerry?' said Winnie. 'What are you doing out here? Ssshh-up your big booming voice, you big lummox! There's a rare kind of an owl somewhere nearby, and I've almost caught it!'

'D'you mean that owl that calls backwards?' asked Jerry, offering a little finger to Winnie to help her pull herself back onto her feet.

'Ssshh! Have you seen it, then?'
whispered Winnie. 'I've been calling it,
and it's been answering me back!'

'Me too!' said Jerry.

'Ssshh! You too what?' asked Winnie.

'I've been calling "twooo twit",
and that owl, it's been calling back
to me, and . . . '

'Twooo twit?! You mean . . . ! Oh!'
Winnie thumped Jerry hard. **Oooph!**
'That wasn't the owl! That was me calling
back, you great steaming great noodle!'

'Well, you're a twit too, if you
thought *I* was a bird!' laughed Jerry.

After a moment, Winnie's scowl melted
into a smile. 'We could try being birds, if
you like,' she said. 'D'you fancy flying,
Jerry?' Before Jerry could say a thing,
Winnie waved her wand. *Abracadabra!*

271

Next instant, Winnie and Jerry felt
something hanging from their shoulders.
They shrugged and found that the heavy
somethings opened and closed behind
them, pushing them forward.

'Eh? Wings, real wings!' said Jerry.
He flip-flap-lurched up onto tiptoe,
then up so that his big boots lifted off
the ground. 'I'm flipping well flying,
missus! I'm flittering and fluttering
like a blooming butterfly!'

Jerry's wings were beautifully patterned, but butterflies don't usually weigh ten tonnes and kick and punch the air as they fly.

Winnie was up in the sky too. Her wings were black tatty bat wings, like old umbrellas. Up went Winnie.

'Weeee! I can loop the loop! I can fly upside down!'

Down below, Wilbur had come out of the house and was watching. He covered his eyes as Winnie looped. He wound a paw claw around his head to show that he thought she was as loopy as her loop. But Winnie was enjoying herself. 'Look at me! I'm going to land in a tree!'

But Jerry got to the tree first. **Crump!** He landed on a branch. It was Scruff who covered his eyes this time. There was a second of quiet, then **creeeeeak** ... **CRASH!** Scruff covered his ears as the branch—and Jerry the butterfly—landed on the ground.

'Oh,' said Jerry. 'Ouch!' said Jerry, rubbing his bottom.

274

A very cross, very ordinary owl, rose up from the tree.

'Twit twoo!' he called.

'Twit yourself!' said Winnie, coming down to land. 'Ah, all that fresh air has given me an appetite. D'you know what I fancy?'

Wilbur shook his head.

'What?' said Jerry.

'I fancy anything at all as long as it doesn't taste of caterpillar!' said Winnie. 'Would you like some jars of caterpillar jam, Jerry?'

'Er . . .'

'On mushroom bread, and with a nice cup of puddle tea? I've got pots of the stuff going free if you'd like it. I think Wilbur and I are going to open a nice tin of tripe.'

'Purrrr!' went Wilbur, and he licked his lips.

271

Who's the boss of the hankies?

The hankie chief.

Where do hangmen look for jobs?

In the noosepaper.

What's a hangman's favourite TV programme?

Noose at Ten.

Wilma's broken my doll.

How did she do that?

I hit her with it.

What would you do with a sick wasp?

Take it to a waspital.

What do you get if you jump in the River Nile?

Wet.

Have you seen an abominable snowman?

Not yeti.

What do you call two corpses in a belfry?

Dead ringers.

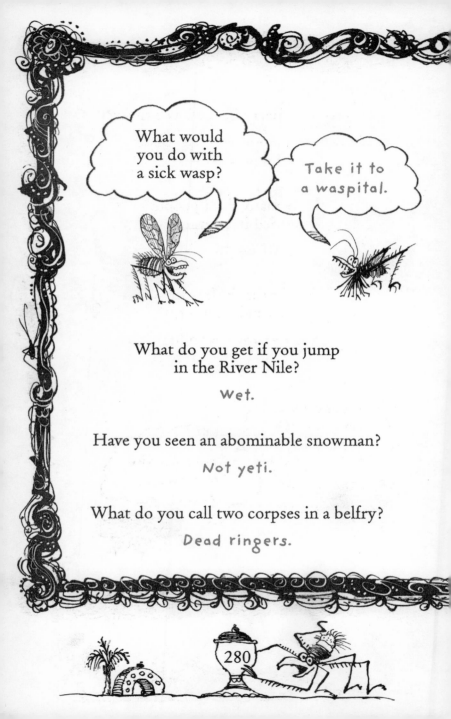

280

Can a man marry his widow's sister?

No, he'd have to be dead
to have a widow.

How many dead people
are buried in a cemetery?

All of them.

What lies at the bottom of
the sea and whimpers?

A nervous wreck.

What do you
do if the M6
is closed?

Drive up the
M3 twice.

Knock Knock

Who's there?

A man who can't reach the doorbell.

Knock Knock

Who's there?

Sadie

Sadie who?

Sadie magic words.

Knock Knock

Who's there?

Madge

Madge who?

Madge E. Quand.

Knock Knock

Who's there?

Arfer

Arfer who?

Arfer got.

Knock Knock

Who's there?

Wand

Wand who?

Wand to come in?

Wilbur

Winnie the Witch

Doctor Which

The Little Ordinaries

Uncle Owen

Mrs Parmar

Jerry the Giant

Cousin Cuthbert

Auntie Alice

The Shopkeeper

Great Aunt Winifred

Enjoy more magic moments with
Winnie AND **Wilbur**